MARVIN REDPOST

Class President

LOUIS SACHAR

MARVIN REDPOST

Class President

illustrated by
Sue Hellard

BLOOMSBURY

LONDON BERLIN NEW YORK

First published in Great Britain in 2004 by Bloomsbury Publishing Plc
This edition published in June 2010 by Bloomsbury Publishing Plc,
36 Soho Square, London W1D 3QY

First published in the U.S.A. in 1999 by
Random House, Inc., New York

Text copyright © 1999 by Louis Sachar
Illustrations copyright © 2004 by Sue Hellard
The moral rights of the author and illustrator have been asserted

A CIP catalogue record for this book
is available from the British Library

ISBN 978 1 4088 0168 0

1 3 5 7 9 10 8 6 4 2

Mixed Sources
Product group from well-managed
forests and other controlled sources
www.fsc.org Cert no. SGS-COC-2061
© 1996 Forest Stewardship Council
FSC

Printed in Great Britain by Clays Ltd, St Ives plc, Bungay, Suffolk

www.louissachar.co.uk
www.bloomsbury.com

1

There was a red post out in front of
Marvin Redpost's house. The rest of the
fence was white. Marvin tapped the post
for luck as he walked through the gate on
his way to school.

He wore a pair of blue jeans with a
hole over each knee. It was "hole day" at
school.

Every day had been special this week.
Monday, he had to wear socks that didn't
match. Tuesday, everyone wore T-shirts
that came from a vacation. Wednesday,
yesterday, had been hat day. And today,

everyone had to wear clothes with holes.

His two best friends, Nick and Stuart, were waiting for him at the corner.

"Do you think Mrs. North will wear clothes with holes?" asked Stuart.

"Sure, why not?" asked Marvin.

"No way!" said Nick. "I'll bet you a million dollars!"

Nick had also said there was "no way!" Mrs. North would wear mismatched socks.

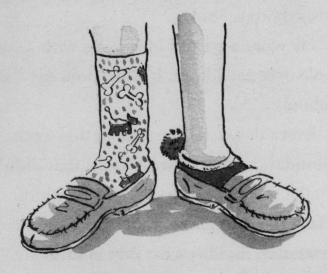

He had also said there was "no way!" she
would let the kids wear hats in class.

So far, he owed Marvin two million dollars.

Nick was wearing a T-shirt that had a large hole under his right armpit. It had been torn in a fight.

"She probably doesn't even own any clothes with holes," Nick said. "How could a teacher get holes in her clothes?"

"Moths," said Marvin. "She might have a wool sweater. Moths eat wool."

"Actually, moths don't really eat wool," Stuart pointed out. "Everybody thinks that, but really, it's the caterpillars that eat the wool."

Stuart was wearing a T-shirt that also had a large hole under the right armpit. It had also been torn in a fight.

It was the same fight.

Nick and Stuart had fought each other. But now they were friends.

"You want to come over after school today?" Nick asked.

"Okay," said Stuart.

"I can't," said Marvin. "My mom is

taking me to the shoe store. I'm going to my cousin's bar mitzvah on Saturday."

When they got to school, everybody they saw had holes in their clothes. Travis wore a shirt that was more hole than it was shirt. Clarence had a hole in his sneaker and his sock, so his big toe stuck all the way through.

"You should clip your toenail," said
Marvin.

"You should clip your mouth!" said
Clarence.

That didn't really make sense, but
Marvin got the point. Clarence was the
toughest kid in his class.

The bell rang, and everybody lined up
and went inside.

Mrs. North was waiting in the class-room. She had a large hole in her shirt, over her stomach.

Marvin stopped and stared. He could see Mrs. North's belly button.

Nick now owed him three million dollars.

2

Casey Happleton usually sat at the desk next to Marvin. She was absent today.

Marvin was disappointed to see her desk empty. She was a funny girl, and he knew she would have liked "hole day."

"I must say," said Mrs. North, "you are all so well dressed today. I've never seen a better-looking group of third graders."

Everybody laughed.

"How'd you get a hole in your shirt?" Kenny asked.

"I was working in my garden," said

Mrs. North. "My shirt got snagged on a thorn from a rosebush."

Marvin nodded. He should have guessed.

"We should dress this way all the time," said Judy Jasper. "That way, nobody would feel bad if their parents were too poor to buy them new clothes."

"That's a good idea," said Mrs. North.

Marvin thought so, too.

"And the holes keep you cool on a hot day," Stuart pointed out.

"You're right," said Mrs. North.

Marvin agreed. Holes made perfect sense. He wondered why nobody had thought of it before.

A child's voice came over the P.A. system. "Please rise for the Pledge of Allegiance."

Every day, a different kid got to lead the school in the pledge.

"That's Casey!" said Judy Jasper.

Marvin recognized Casey's voice as she recited the pledge. She sounded very serious.

He put his hand over his heart and said it along with her.

When Casey came back to class, she told Mrs. North that Mr. McCabe wanted to see her. Mr. McCabe was the principal.

"Did he say why?" Mrs. North asked.

Casey shook her head.

Casey wore a shirt that was way too big for her. Marvin guessed it was her father's. Not only did it have holes in it, but it also had paint spilled on it.

Mrs. North told the class she would be gone for only a minute. She said she expected everyone to behave and to use their time wisely.

After she left, Nick said, "I bet you Mrs. North got in trouble for wearing torn clothes!"

"No, Mr. McCabe is also wearing torn clothes," said Casey. "I saw his elbow."

"What did it look like?" asked Judy.

"Pink and bumpy," said Casey.

Casey had a ponytail that stuck out of the side of her head instead of the back. She sat down next to Marvin. The ponytail was on Marvin's side. Sometimes, when Casey laughed really hard, her ponytail went around in circles.

Mrs. North was gone for a lot longer than a minute. When she returned, she had a very strange expression on her face. She looked lost. She opened her mouth, but didn't say anything.

"Are you all right?" asked Kenny.

Mrs. North looked at Kenny, but still didn't say anything. Finally, she spoke. She said, "We are ..." then stopped.

She started again. "There will ..."

That was as far as she got.

She tried again. "I expect ..."

Her mouth shut tight. She tapped her desk with her fist.

At last she managed to say a complete sentence. "We are going to have a visitor today."

Marvin couldn't wait to hear who it was. From the way Mrs. North was acting, he thought it must be somebody weird.

"Who is it?" asked Warren.

"Is it somebody I've heard of?" asked Nick.

"Oh, I hope so, Nick," said Mrs. North. Then she took a deep breath and said, "The president will be coming here."

Everybody gasped.

Marvin was a little confused. He wasn't sure which president Mrs. North meant. Did she mean the president of the United States? Or did she mean the president of something else, like the president of a shoe company?

Marvin's school was in Maryland. It was less than twenty miles from Washington, D.C. His father worked in Washington, D.C. So it was possible that Mrs. North meant the president of the United States. But why would the president of the United States come to his school?

He raised his hand.

Pasty Gatsby raised her hand, too.

"Yes, Patsy," said Mrs. North.

"The president of what?" Patsy asked.

Mrs. North stared at her as if she thought Patsy was an alien from another planet. "The president of the United States," she said.

"Duh!" said Travis.

Patsy blushed.

"Sometimes I wonder about you, Patsy," said Mrs. North.

"What'd you think? The president of Mexico?" asked Clarence.

Marvin turned red, too, but nobody noticed. He lowered his hand.

"Yes, Marvin, did you have a question?" asked Mrs. North.

He shook his head. "No, I was just stretching."

Mrs. North explained that even Mr. McCabe hadn't known the president was coming until ten minutes ago. It had been kept secret for security reasons.

"Now, I know I don't have to tell you how to behave when the president gets here," she said.

Then she told everybody how to behave.

"Be respectful. Be attentive. If you get a chance to speak to him, remember to speak loud and clear. You should call him 'Mr. President.' 'Yes, Mr. President.' 'Thank you, Mr. President.' Remember to—"

Mrs. North suddenly stopped talking. "Oh, my gosh!" she exclaimed. "I have to change my clothes!"

3

Mrs. North didn't know what time the president would come. So she couldn't go home and change out of her torn clothes.

"I hope it's not during recess," said Nick.

"We'll adjust our schedule," Mrs. North assured him.

"Good, because I don't want to miss recess," said Nick.

While they waited for the president to show up, Mrs. North told everyone to write down a question he or she would like to ask the president.

"Like what?" asked Nick.

"Anything," said Mrs. North. Then she looked at Nick and said, "Well, not *anything*. There must be something you're curious about, Nick. What's it like to live in the White House? What does he have for breakfast? Does he ever just sit around and watch TV? Think, Nick." She tapped on the side of her head with her finger. "Use your brain."

Marvin tried
to think, too.

He remembered
that he was going
shopping for new
shoes right after
school, along with his
brother and sister.

He wondered if the
president bought his
own clothes. It would be
pretty strange, he thought,
for the president just to
walk into a store and try on
a pair of shoes. But if
someone else bought them for
him, they might not fit. Or
he might not like the
color.

31

He wrote down his question.

Do you buy your own shoes?

No, that's stupid, he decided. He
thought he should ask the president
something more important. He should ask
about war or pollution.

He tried to erase what he wrote.

He looked over at Casey. She had her

finger in her mouth. Then she took it out,
picked up her pencil, and wrote very fast.
She laughed, then wrote some more.

It was a long question. Her ponytail
bounced up and down.

"What will you ask him?" Marvin
asked.

"I'm not telling you," said Casey.

Marvin wrote down a new question:

Are we going to get into a war anytime soon?

He hadn't done a very good job erasing the old question. His paper was messy and hard to read. He hoped the president wouldn't see it.

"Does spelling count?" asked Judy.

"You're not being graded on this," said Mrs. North. "It's not a test. It's an opportunity. Try to make the most of it."

Clarence raised his hand and asked, "Does the president have a dog?"

"Um, I don't know," said Mrs. North. "But that might be—"

"I want to ask him his dog's name," said Clarence. "But first I have to know if he has a dog, don't I?"

"Well, why don't you ask him if he has

any pets?" suggested Mrs. North.

"Oh, yeah," said Clarence. "Thanks."

Marvin wrote down his second question: *What are you doing about pollution?*

He was still trying to think of a third question when the classroom door opened.

Marvin dropped his pencil.

4

A tall man stepped into the classroom.

Marvin stared at him in awe. He was pretty sure it was the president. He was certain he'd seen the man's face on the news.

Marvin's father watched the news every evening before dinner.

The man was tall and wore a suit and tie. He looked very important.

Behind him was a woman carrying a big camera. CHANNEL 2 was printed in big letters on the camera.

Marvin stood up. He put his hand on

his heart, as if he was saying the Pledge of Allegiance. He could feel his heartbeat.

"Are you the president?" asked Kenny.

The man laughed. So did the woman holding the camera.

"What an idiot," said Heather.

"Don't you even know what the president looks like?" said Gina.

"Duh!" said Nick.

Kenny blushed.

"Marvin, why are you standing?" asked Mrs. North.

"Uh, just stretching," said Marvin. He sat back down.

"Did you get that on camera?" the man asked the camera woman.

"No," she said.

"All right, let's do it again," said the man. "I'll walk in again, and you ..." he pointed to Kenny. "What's your name?"

"Kenny," said Kenny.

"I'll walk in again, and Kenny, you ask me if I'm the president. And try to look cute."

Kenny seemed very confused.

"No, he will not," said Mrs. North.

The man looked at Mrs. North's belly button. "Who are you?" he asked.

"I am Mrs. North. This is my classroom. Who are you?"

The man seemed surprised she didn't know. "I am Clark Rogers from Channel Two News."

"Well, Mr. Rogers," said Mrs. North. "I do not like the way you walked in without knocking. You disturbed my class. And I don't want you embarrassing any of my students on television. Now, if you want to stay, you may wait, *quietly*,

40

in the back of the room. Otherwise you
will have to leave."

Clark Rogers stared at her a moment. Mrs. North stared right back at him.

"Sorry," he said. He and the camera woman moved to the back of the room.

Marvin felt very proud of his teacher.

More news people came from other TV
stations. They all crowded into the back
of the room. There were three television
cameras, and also a photographer from
the newspaper.

Mrs. North went ahead with the
arithmetic lesson.

They'd been learning to add big
numbers. Mrs. North put a problem on
the board.

She said the numbers out loud. "Sixty-
three million, eight hundred and eighty-
eight thousand, two hundred and twenty-
seven *plus* seventeen million, one hundred

and six thousand, five hundred and forty-seven."

Marvin's mouth dropped open. He had never heard anyone add such big numbers.

"Marvin," said Mrs. North, "would

you like to come to the board and give us the answer?"

He closed his mouth.

Then he stood up and made his way to the board. He looked at the problem.

It was impossible.

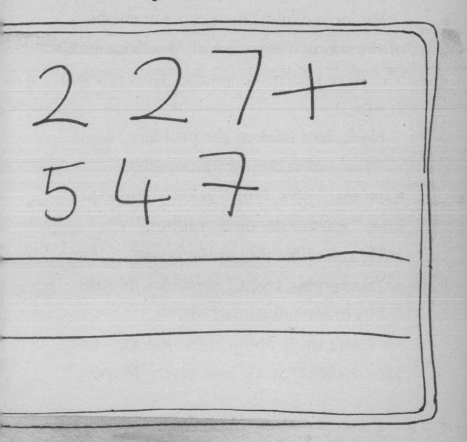

227+
547

Mrs. North gave him a *you-can-do-it* smile.

He looked at all the people at the back of the room. They were all watching him. The three television cameras were pointed at him.

He looked back at the problem.

"You add it up just like smaller numbers," Mrs. North gently reminded him. "Start at the ones column."

He stared blankly at the board.

"Seven plus seven," said Mrs. North.

His brain had turned off.

"Don't think about the cameras," said Mrs. North. "Seven plus seven, Marvin."

Marvin looked around helplessly. Casey Happleton was making funny faces at him.

She stretched her mouth in different directions.

He thought she was making fun of him.

Then he realized her mouth was forming the word "fourteen" over and over again.

"Fourteen," he said.

"Good," said Mrs. North.

He wrote the number four and carried the one.

His brain started working again.

"Two plus four is six, plus one is seven." He put seven in the next column.

He carefully went through the problem, one step at a time.

He was almost finished when there was a knock at the door.

Mr. McCabe, the principal, opened the door and said, "Excuse us. Do you mind if we come in?"

Another man was with him.

Marvin was pretty sure the other man was the president.

Mrs. North said, "W-w-w-welcome."
She wiggled her hand behind her back,
signaling the class to stand.

Marvin was already standing, but he
stood straighter.

Everyone clapped as the other man
walked into the classroom.

"Thank you," he said. "Please sit down."

Marvin didn't know what to do. He didn't want to disobey the president. But he had been standing before the president came.

"This is Mrs. North," said Mr. McCabe.

Mr. McCabe wore a long-sleeve shirt. He had a hole over his pink and bony elbow.

"I've heard wonderful things about you," the president said. He shook Mrs. North's hand.

Marvin couldn't believe that his teacher was really shaking the president's hand.

"Thank you," said Mrs. North. "I've heard—I mean—we are all delighted you are here."

The president turned and looked at Marvin. "Those are big numbers," he said.

Marvin didn't know what to say.

"Did you add those by yourself?"

"It's not finished," said Marvin.

The president smiled. "Well, go ahead, finish."

Marvin took a breath and exhaled. He looked back at the problem on the board. He'd lost his place. He had to start back at the beginning and add the numbers in his head.

He finished the problem.

The president looked it over. "What's your name?" he asked.

"Um ..." Marvin's brain had turned off again, but then it came back on. "Marvin. Marvin Redpost."

"Good job, Marvin," said the president. He held out his hand.

Marvin shook hands with the president.

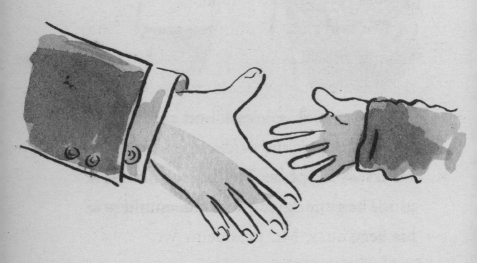

6

Marvin returned to his desk.

"Thank you for letting me come and interrupt your class," the president said. "I won't stay too long. I don't want you to miss recess." He smiled.

"We don't care!" shouted Stuart. "Stay as long as you want."

Mrs. North gave The Look to Stuart.

"Mrs. North said we'll get recess after you go away," said Nick.

Mrs. North gave The Look to Nick, too. Then she said, "We understand you are very busy, Mr. President. We appreciate any—"

There was a jar filled with marbles on Mrs. North's desk. As Mrs. North spoke, her hand swept across her desk and knocked the marble jar over. The marbles spilled out, rolled off the desk, and bounced onto the floor.

The children in the front row scrambled to pick up the rolling marbles.

The president helped, too.

Mrs. North's face was as red as the post in front of Marvin's house.

The children put the marbles back in the jar.

"I am *so* sorry," said Mrs. North.

The president dropped two marbles into the jar, *plop, plop*, and said, "No problem."

Everyone settled back into their seats.

"You are probably wondering why I've

come here today," the president said.

Marvin had been wondering that.

"Well, I want to talk about what it means to be a good citizen. Who knows what a citizen is?"

Lots of hands went up in the air.

Marvin didn't raise his hand. He thought he knew what a citizen was, but

he didn't know how to say it.

"Yes?" said the president, looking at
Melanie.

"A person," said Melanie.

"Very good answer," said the president.
"A citizen is a person. But is there a
difference between a person and a
citizen?"

Melanie shrugged.

"Anyone know?" asked the president.

Some hands started to go up, but then came back down.

Clarence raised his hand.

"Yes," said the president.

"Do you have a dog?" asked Clarence.

"Yes, I do," said the president, "but that's not what we're talking about now."

Mrs. North gave The Look to Clarence.

"Who can tell me the difference between a person and a citizen?" the president asked. "How about you, Marvin?"

Marvin couldn't believe it. The president had remembered his name!

He tried to come up with an answer. He didn't want to let the president down. "Um, well, if you're a person, it's like

you're alone. A citizen is part of
something bigger, like a country?"

He didn't know if that made sense or
not.

"Exactly right!" said the president. "We are not alone. We are all part of a big group. That group is called the United States of America."

Marvin smiled. He wasn't sure if that was what he had meant when he said it, but it made sense when the president said it.

"America is not just a place on a map,"

the president said. "America is made up of all of its citizens. If we want America to be a great country, it is up to every single one of us—me, you, Mr. McCabe, Mrs. North, Marvin—to be good citizens."

The president asked the students if they could think of ways to be good citizens.

Casey Happleton raised her hand.

"Yes, ma'am," said the president.

Casey smiled, then got serious again. "Help people who need help," she said.

"Very good."

Nick raised his hand.

"Yes, sir," said the president.

"Don't fight," said Nick.

"Excellent," said the president.

Lots of hands went up in the air.

"Clean up after yourself," said Travis.

"Recycle," said Patsy.

"Brush your teeth," said Gina.

The president had to think about that one. "It's important for citizens to try to be clean and healthy," he agreed.

Marvin thought of some good ideas, too, but he didn't raise his hand. He'd already gotten to shake the president's hand. He wanted to let others have a

chance. That was part of being a good
citizen.

Nearly everybody in the class came up
with something: Listen to your teacher
and parents. Don't make fun of people.
Put out fires. Don't cheat. Don't lie. Smile.

The president said he was very
impressed with all the ideas the children
had.

"This is why I wanted to come to a third-grade class," he said. "I knew third graders would know how to be good citizens. Sometimes, when people get older, they forget. I hope a lot of people will see and hear you on television this evening. They may learn something."

7

"If you have time, Mr. President, the children have prepared questions," said Mrs. North.

"Well, I hope I'm prepared to answer them," said the president. "Now that I've met your class, I'm sure they will be very interesting questions."

Mrs. North had the students take turns coming to the front of the room. They would go by rows.

Marvin sat in the fourth seat of the second row. He counted the people ahead of him. He would be ninth.

Judy Jasper was first.

Mrs. North told her to first say her name and then ask her question. She reminded her to speak loud enough for everyone to hear.

"Judy Jasper!" shouted Judy, causing the president to jump back.

"Not quite so loud," said Mrs. North.

"Judy Jasper," said Judy. "When you were in the third grade, did you know you would be president someday?"

"When I was in the third grade, Judy,"
said the president. "I don't think I even
knew there *was* a president. I was more
interested in playing with my friends."

Judy started to return to her seat, but
the president called her back and shook
her hand.

Stuart was next. "Stuart Albright," he said. "What if you don't like white? Can you paint your house a different color?"

The president laughed.

"The White House doesn't belong to me. I live there, but it belongs to all of the citizens of our country. And I don't think they'd like it if I painted it blue with yellow polka dots. Do you, Stuart?"

Stuart's mouth dropped open. "Uh, I, uh, um, it's okay with me."

He shook the president's hand and hurried back to his seat.

Marvin practiced his question in his head. *What are you doing about pollution?* He wondered if he had to say his name first, since the president already knew it. *Marvin Redpost. What are you doing about pollution, Mr. President?* He had to remember to call him Mr. President.

Clarence was next. "I have a two-part question," he said.

"Okay," said the president.

"Do you have a dog?"

"Yes."

"Does your dog know you're the president?"

The president laughed. "You know, Clarence, I've been asked lots of questions, but I don't think anyone has ever asked me that before." He thought it over, then said, "I don't think my dog cares if I'm president. I've had Pickles for twelve years. She has always made me feel as if I was the most special person in the whole world. Even before I was president."

Clarence shook the president's hand.

"Casey Happleton. Are you doing anything to get rid of pollution, Mr. President?"

Marvin felt a stab of disappointment.
Now he had to think of another question.
"I'm trying," said the president.

"The problem is that everyone causes a tiny bit of pollution. Everybody thinks their little bit doesn't make any difference. But when you put all those tiny bits together, you get a big problem."

Casey nodded.

"Ask your other question!" said Melanie.

"Only one question each," said Mrs. North.

"But she's got a question I bet he's never heard before," said Melanie.

"Well, let's hear it," said the president.

Casey looked at Mrs. North to see if it was okay. In the classroom, Mrs. North was still the boss. Not the president.

Mrs. North nodded.

Casey took a breath. "Do I have to say my name again?"

"No, I know you're Casey Happleton,"
said the president.

Casey smiled. She took another breath.
"If a spaceship lands in my backyard and
a little green man says, 'Take me to your
leader,' should I take him to you? And
how do I do that?"

Everybody laughed.

"I think you should take him to Mrs. North," said the president.

Everybody laughed again. Mrs. North laughed the loudest.

Casey shook the president's hand.

Marvin practiced his war question. *Marvin Redpost. Are we going to get into a war anytime soon, Mr. President? Marvin Redpost. Are we ...*

It was Travis's turn. "Hi, I'm Travis. Do you hate people who didn't vote for you?"

"No. What really bothers me, Travis, is

when people don't vote at all. It makes me think they don't care about their country."

"Oh, good," said Travis. "Because my parents voted. They just didn't vote for you."

The president shook his hand.

"Patsy Gatsby," said Patsy. She was the first person in Marvin's row. "Are there ever days when you wish you weren't president?"

The president had to think a long time before answering that one. "I know there are days when *other people* wish I wasn't president," he said.

"Like Travis's parents," said Patsy.

The president smiled. "It's not an easy job, Patsy," he said. "There are times when it would be nice to take a hike, or just watch TV, or something. But I don't think I've ever wished I wasn't president. I feel very proud to have been elected to serve the citizens of this country."

Patsy shook his hand, then returned to her seat.

"Nick Tuffle. When you go to another country, do you ever have to eat really weird food and pretend you like it?"

The president nodded. "It happens a lot. I try to spread it around on my plate, so it looks as if I ate more than I really did."

"I do that, too," said Nick. "What's the weirdest thing you ever had to eat?"

"Probably jellyfish."

"Oh, gross!" said Nick.

Nick didn't seem at all nervous talking to the president. They shook hands, then he returned to his seat.

Marvin was getting very nervous. It was Melanie's turn, and he was after Melanie. *Mr. President. Are we going to get into a war anytime soon? Marvin Redpost.*

Melanie asked her question. "Is there going to be another war?"

Marvin couldn't believe it.

"I hope not, Melanie. It's just like being a good citizen. You shouldn't fight. Our country is a citizen of the world. And we shouldn't fight either."

Melanie shook the president's hand.

Marvin slowly walked to the front of the room.

"Hi, Marvin," said the president. "I'm sure you've got a real good question."

Marvin didn't know what to do. All he had left was his shoe question. "Marvin

Redpost," he said. He looked at the president, who was looking at him. Marvin was impressed by how kind and smart he was, and how he remembered everybody's name. Marvin hoped to be president someday, too, and he wanted to be just like him. "Is there something we should be doing now if we want to be president someday?"

The president nodded and smiled at Marvin. "I think you're already doing it, Marvin," he said. "Work hard. Listen to your teacher. Be a good citizen. All those things we talked about earlier. If you do that, then any one of you—Casey, Travis, Nick, Patsy—might be president someday."

The president put his arm around Marvin's shoulders. "Take a good look at this bright young man here. You may be looking at a future president."

Marvin could see all the cameras were pointed at him and the president. He tried not to smile. He didn't want to look goofy.

8

The president left. The television crews
left. Mr. McCabe returned to the
principal's office.

"Well," said Mrs. North.

That was all she said.

Everyone waited for her to say more.

"Well, well, well," said Mrs. North.

She walked from one end of the room
to the other, then back again.

Marvin's head was spinning. He
couldn't wait to get home and tell his
parents that the president had said he
might be president someday.

"You guys were terrific!" Mrs. North

said at last. "I have never been so proud."

"Was I a good citizen?" asked Clarence.

"Yes, Clarence, you were," said Mrs. North. "You *all* were."

"Did we earn a marble?" asked Gina.

When the children were good, Mrs. North would add a marble to the jar on her desk. When the jar was full, they'd get to go to Lake Park.

Mrs. North opened her desk drawer

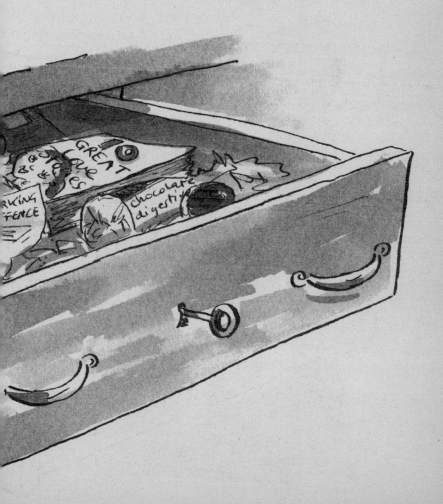

and took out her bag of marbles. She
pulled out a handful of marbles and
dropped them in the jar.

    Plop ploppity, ploppity plop.

"Let's go to Lake Park!" she said.

Everyone cheered.

On the way to the park, Marvin spoke
to Casey. "Thanks for helping me on the
math problem."

"I knew you knew it," said Casey.
"Your brain just got stuck."

Marvin smiled. He thought Casey was
a good citizen.

If Casey hadn't helped him, then he never would have gotten the problem right, and the president wouldn't have told him he might be president someday.

He decided that when he got to be president, he would ask Casey to be vice president.

Just so long as nobody thought he liked her.

He wondered if she would still have a ponytail sticking out of the side of her head.

Stuart came up alongside him. "Lake Park on a Thursday! Can you believe it?"

Usually, they only got to go to Lake Park on Fridays.

Marvin couldn't even remember what day it was anymore.

"Hey, you guys want to come over to my house after school?" asked Nick.

"Sure," said Stuart.

"How about you, Marvin?"

Marvin really wanted to go home and

tell his family about the president. But he knew his parents wouldn't get home until after five o'clock, anyway. They both worked.

"Sure, okay," he said.

He stumbled, but caught his balance. He looked down at his feet. He had a strange feeling, as if his feet were trying to tell him something.

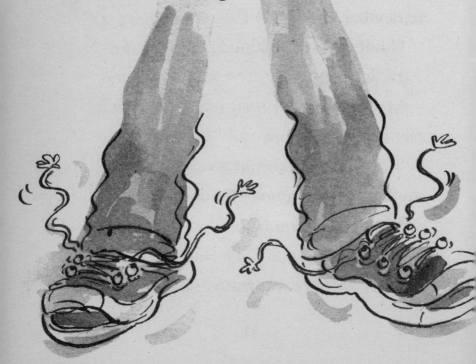

9

Marvin came home late in the afternoon.
He was tired from playing hard, but still
very excited. He walked through the gate,
past the red post. Suddenly, he
remembered.

"Shoes," he said aloud.

He felt awful. It seemed as if he was
always forgetting something. He sighed.
He knew his mom would be mad. She
had planned to leave work early just so
she could take him shopping.

Maybe she forgot, too, he thought. He
hoped.

Linzy, his little sister, met him at the

door. "You better hide," she warned.

Marvin slowly stepped inside.

His mother was standing by the stairs. Her hands were on her hips. "So nice of you to come home," she said.

"Sorry," said Marvin.

"Sorry?" asked his mother. "Is that it?"

Marvin didn't know what else he could say. "I forgot," he said. "You won't believe what happened at school today!"

"What was the last thing I said to you before you left this morning?" his mother asked.

Marvin sighed. "You said to come straight home so we could go shopping for shoes. But—"

"I left work early so that I would be able to take you," said his mother. "I had to rearrange my whole work schedule."

Marvin's father came down the stairs. "Don't you ever think about others?" he asked.

It was two against one.

"Linzy, Jacob, and your mother sat around waiting for you," his father said. "Don't you think they had better things to do?"

"I'm sorry," Marvin said again. "I forgot all about it. But you won't—"

"We finally left without you," said his

mother. "Now I'm going to have to take you to the store tomorrow. Which means rearranging my work schedule *again*."

"I can wear my old shoes," Marvin offered.

"Maybe you should just go barefoot to your cousin's bar mitzvah," said his father. "Maybe that will help you learn."

"Can I go barefoot, too?" asked Jacob. He smiled at Marvin.

Their parents didn't think that was funny.

"Do you know what time it is?" his mother asked him.

"No."

"It's almost six o'clock," said his father.

"Six o'clock?" asked Marvin. "Quick, turn on the TV!"

His parents stared at him. His mother raised her eyebrows. "There will be no television for you," said his father. "Not for a week. Maybe then you won't forget so much. Maybe television is destroying your brain."

"It's not regular television," Marvin tried to explain. "The—"

"No TV!" shouted his mother.

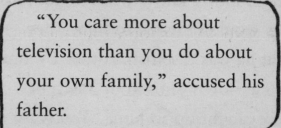

"You care more about television than you do about your own family," accused his father.

"I don't," said Marvin. "But you have to watch—"

"We don't have to watch anything!" his mother interrupted. "Now, I don't want to hear any more about it. If you keep it up, there will be no TV for a month. You may go to your room and get started on your homework."

Marvin didn't know what to do. His parents wouldn't listen to him. They thought he was a selfish, rotten TV mushbrain. He slowly started up the stairs.

Linzy caught up to him. "You want to see my new shoes, Marvin? They're really pretty. They have bows and buttons."

Marvin tried to smile.

Down below, in the family room, Marvin's father turned on the news. Marvin heard Clark Roger's voice coming from the television.

"The president went looking for good

citizens today. And he found them at
Dogwood Elementary School."
Marvin stopped.

"Hey, Marvin, that's your school!" Jacob shouted from the bottom of the stairs.

"That's Marvin!" exclaimed Marvin's father.

"I want to see!" said Linzy. She ran down the stairs.

Marvin stepped down a couple of steps and leaned way over the banister. He saw himself on TV adding the big numbers. Then he saw the president talking to his class.

"America is not just a place on a map.

America is made up of all of its citizens. If we want America to be a great country, it is up to every single one of us—me, you, Mr. McCabe, Mrs. North, Marvin— to be good citizens."

"Did he mean you, Marvin?" asked Jacob.

"Shh!" said Marvin's mother.

"The students in Mrs. North's third-grade class had lots of ideas about what it means to be a good citizen," said Clark Rogers.

Marvin saw Casey Happleton on the television.

"Help people who need help."

"There's Nick," said Jacob.

"Don't fight."

"And Stuart," said Marvin's mother. *"If you, uh, see a fire or something, you should put it out."*

"The students also had lots of interesting and unusual questions for the president," said Clark Rogers.

Marvin heard Kenny ask, *"Do you ever mess up? You know, make mistakes?"* He hoped his parents listened to the president's answer.

"Of course. Everybody makes mistakes. And when you're president, you can really mess up big time. But if you're smart, you learn from your mistakes. And you should try to be understanding and forgive other people when they make mistakes."

Marvin nearly fell over the banister, but caught himself.

"The children in Mrs. North's class were very impressed with their visitor, and I think the president was very impressed with the children," said Clark Rogers.

"There's Marvin!" screamed Linzy.

Marvin strained to look.

"Is there something we should be doing now if we want to be president someday?"

"I think you're already doing it, Marvin. Work hard. Listen to your teacher. Be a good citizen. All those things we talked about earlier. If you do that, then any one of you—Casey, Travis, Nick, Patsy—might be president someday.

"Take a good look at this bright young man here. You may be looking at a future president."

Marvin's parents looked at Marvin, first on TV, then on the stairs.

Maybe he wasn't so bad after all.

About the Author

Louis Sachar lives in Austin, Texas, with his wife, Carla, their daughter, Sherre, and their two dogs, Lucky and Tippy. In his spare time Louis likes to play bridge. Carla likes to read. Sherre likes to play with her friends. Lucky likes to catch Frisbees. Tippy likes to chew up shoes, fan letters, and Sherre's favorite toys. They all try to be good citizens, except, perhaps, Tippy.